For my children: Jeff, Joe, Sean, Nick, and Hannah.
And for my mother, Laura K. Griswell, who taught me to read
and to love books long before I started school. –K. T. G.

For my daughter, Sasha, and my son, Kostya. –V. G.

STERLING CHILDREN'S BOOKS
New York
An Imprint of Sterling Publishing
387 Park Avenue South
New York, NY 10016

STERLING CHILDREN'S BOOKS and the distinctive Sterling Children's Books logo are trademarks
of Sterling Publishing Co., Inc.

Text © 2013 by Kim T. Griswell
Illustrations © 2013 by Valeri Gorbachev
The artwork for this book was created using ink and watercolor.
Designed by Jennifer Browning

ISBN 978-1-4549-0416-8

Library of Congress Cataloging-in-Publication Data

Griswell, Kim T.
Rufus goes to school / by Kim T. Griswell : illustrated by Valeri Gorbachev.
    p. cm.
Summary: Rufus Leroy Williams III wants to go to school to learn to read but the principal at first refuses because Rufus is a pig.
ISBN 978-1-4549-0416-8
[1. Books and reading--Fiction. 2. Pigs--Fiction. 3. School principals--Fiction. 4. Schools--Fiction.] I. Gorbachev, Valeri, ill. II. Title.
PZ7.G88797Ruf 2013
[E]--dc23

                      2012035510

Distributed in Canada by Sterling Publishing
c/o Canadian Manda Group, 165 Dufferin Street
Toronto, Ontario, Canada M6K 3H6
Distributed in the United Kingdom by GMC Distribution Services
Castle Place, 166 High Street, Lewes, East Sussex, England BN7 1XU
Distributed in Australia by Capricorn Link (Australia) Pty. Ltd.
P.O. Box 704, Windsor, NSW 2756, Australia

For information about custom editions, special sales, and premium and corporate purchases, please contact
Sterling Special Sales at 800-805-5489 or specialsales@sterlingpublishing.com.

Manufactured in China
Lot #:
2 4 6 8 10 9 7 5 3 1
5/13

www.sterlingpublishing.com/kids

Rufus Goes to School

by
Kim T. Griswell

illustrated by
Valeri Gorbachev

STERLING CHILDREN'S BOOKS
New York

Every day, Rufus Leroy Williams III turned the pages of his favorite book. He looked at every picture. He made up stories to go with them. But he could not read the words.

Rufus knew just what to do. He would go to school and learn to read. But first, he needed a backpack.

Early the next morning, Rufus scuttled down the street to school. He peeked through the front door.

Then he trotted down the hall to the principal's office. He was greeted by the principal's secretary.

Principal Lipid's secretary knocked on his door. "There's a pig to see you."

Rufus stepped forward. "My name is Rufus Leroy Williams III," he said. "I have a backpack, and I am ready for school."

The principal shook his head.
"No pigs in school!"

"Why not?" asked Rufus.

"Because pigs track mud in the halls,"
said Principal Lipid.

"They turn their drawings into airplanes."

"They play leapfrog in class,

and they start food fights in the cafeteria."

Rufus frowned.
"But I have a backpack."

"Makes no difference,"
said Principal Lipid.
And he showed Rufus to the door.

Rufus Leroy Williams III really wanted to go to school.
And he knew just what he needed. "A lunchbox!"

Right before lunchtime, the secretary poked her head into Principal Lipid's office. "The pig is back," she whispered.

"My name is Rufus Leroy Williams III," he said. "I have a backpack and a lunchbox. I am ready for school."

The principal folded his arms. "No pigs in school!"

"Why not?" asked Rufus.

"Because pigs knock over the block towers,"
said Principal Lipid,

"and they hide under the teacher's desk."

"Pigs draw stick figures on the chalkboard." He waggled his finger at Rufus.

"And they chase their classmates during recess."

"But I have a backpack *and* a lunchbox!"
Rufus frowned.

"Makes no difference," said Principal Lipid.
And he waved Rufus out the door.

Rufus Leroy Williams III really, really wanted to go to school.
And he knew just what he needed. "A blanket!"

During naptime, the secretary opened Principal Lipid's door. "Sir?"

Rufus Leroy Williams III rushed past her. "I have a backpack, a lunchbox, and a blanket, and now I am *really* ready for school."

The principal sighed. "I told you. No pigs–"

"Wait!" said Rufus.

"I will never blow
bubbles in my milk.

Or finger-paint my classmates."

"I will not stand on my head
during naptime.

Or leave nose prints on the windows.
And I will come to school *every day!*"

"Sorry." The principal shook his head. "No pigs in school."

"But I have a backpack, a lunchbox, *and* a blanket!" said Rufus.

"Is that all?" asked the principal.

Rufus frowned. What else could he need for school?

"I have *this*." Rufus held up his favorite book. "And I want to learn to read it."

"Ah!" Principal Lipid smiled. "That makes a difference!"

He escorted Rufus out of his office and down the hall.

"This is Rufus Leroy Williams III," Principal Lipid announced as they entered a classroom. "And he will be joining your class."

"Hooray!" shouted the boys and girls.

Rufus Leroy Williams III put away his backpack, his lunchbox, his blanket, and his favorite book. He was ready for school.

Rufus loved learning the A, B, Cs
(especially the letter P).

He loved learning the 1, 2, 3s.

He loved lunchtime . . .

and naptime.

But Rufus loved storytime most of all . . .

... because it gave him room to dream.